EURO TOURNAMENT
HOCKEY
WARS 12

SAM LAWRENCE & BEN JACKSON

Illustrations by Tanya Zeinalova

 **Book # 12 - Hockey Wars Series**

www.indiepublishinggroup.com

Every day is a great day for hockey.

—Mario Lemieux

Other Books by Sam & Ben

"I CAN'T BELIEVE it's the last weekend of summer," Rhys said, swiping at a little flower in front of the bench they were sitting on.

"What did that flower do to you?" Georgia said, giving Rhys an evil stare, "imagine if I was a giant and just came along out of nowhere and squished you!"

"I don't think the flower cares," Rhys said laughing, "and you're too slow and clumsy to squish me, even if you were as high as that building over there!"

Before the last word had even left his mouth, Georgia was up and off the bench chasing him. Rhys wasn't silly. He knew what was coming and had taken off across the park, screaming at the top of his voice.

The kids had all had a massive summer, and as usual, it was quickly coming to an end. No doubt too soon if you asked any of them!

"Millie, did you and Cameron go up to the same cabin again this summer?" Khloe asked.

"Yep," Millie replied, "it was awesome. Again. I never get sick of spending time up there. I wonder if I lived there all the time would it be so cool?"

"Probably, it looks pretty nice up there," Khloe replied, "plus, being able to swim in the lake whenever you want and hang out on the deck of the cottage is pretty cool."

"Yeah," Millie said, thinking about the cabin that she, Cameron, and their families had spent two weeks at. "Oh, I forgot to mention it, but they got a new boat this year. So, that was pretty cool. We did a lot more water-skiing, fishing, and stuff. So, what did you get up to, Khloe?"

"Well, we had a big family reunion. We all had to go to my grandparent's house, and a bunch of my family came from all over the country for the long weekend. So that was pretty cool. There were so many kids there that I had never met before," Khloe answered. "Oh, and one of my cousins is a hockey goalie also, so that was pretty funny."

Millie laughed, "Two goalies in the one family. What are the chances? Are they any good?"

"Yeah, she's pretty good but not as good as me," Khloe said with a smirk. "There's only one me."

"Only one me what?" Georgia said, as she plopped herself down on the bench, puffing and a little breathless.

"One goalie as good as Khloe," Cameron replied, filling her in on the conversation she'd missed while chasing Rhys.

"Oh," Georgia said lost, "that is true. I couldn't imagine having two Khloes."

"We were just talking about what we got up to over the summer," Millie said.

"I had the worst summer ever," Rhys said. "It was so bad. You wouldn't believe me if I told you."

"It sounds like you're about to," Cameron said, rolling his eyes.

"Having your account deleted from Fortnite isn't the end of the world," Preston said laughing, "despite what you may think, Rhys. People had way worse summers than that."

"Bro, they 100% just deleted it. All my progress is gone, my skins, items, and everything else!" Rhys said, spinning around. "I'd say that's pretty close to the end of the world."

"Did they say why they deleted it?" Hunter asked.

"Because he got caught cheating!" Cameron said laughing, "so they banned his account."

"That's not what happened!" Rhys shouted, getting angrier and angrier, "I accidentally downloaded this program that this guy online said would help me get better. I didn't know that I couldn't use it, then all of a sudden, my account was deleted. I barely used it! They didn't even give me a warning."

"That's what they do when you get caught cheating," Georgia said laughing. "Just own it, Rhys. Start a new account."

"I did," Rhys said, "still sucks, though."

"What did you get up to, Preston?" Lola asked.

"Well, we went to Hawaii for a couple of weeks," Preston replied, "other than that, not much."

"Other than that," Hunter said casually, "just a quick trip to Hawaii. Like we all just went on a quick trip to a tropical island. How was Hawaii? It looks amazing!"

"I've always wanted to go there," Khloe added, "it looks so pretty."

"It was pretty cool," Preston admitted laughing, "but Mom and Dad were working a lot of the trip, so I spent most of the days just hanging out at the resort alone. It's where I got this awesome tan."

"You do look very tanned," Millie said laughing, "it suits you."

"Thanks," Preston said shyly, "I also got to jump off the big diving board at the pool, which was pretty scary at first."

"You went off the highest board?" Cameron asked, impressed, "that is wild!"

"Yeah, I had to work my way up before jumping off that one," Preston said, pulling out his phone and showing his friends a picture of the pool and diving board and a video of him jumping from the top.

"That's awesome!" They all chorused as they crowded closer to get a look at the video.

The kids hung out in the park for the rest of the afternoon and well into the evening, playing ball hockey and generally just messing around together.

With only a few more days and nights of summer left, they wanted to milk every last minute of fun out of summer before they had to return to school, and the days started getting colder and shorter.

"Do my eyes deceive me?" Cameron said, acting visibly shocked as he walked up the driveway of

Millie's house, "has someone snatched my friend Millie and replaced her with a body double? Have I woken up in a parallel universe where everything is reversed? My world is upside down!"

"Oh, you're so funny," Millie said, rolling her eyes, "I wish we were in a parallel universe. It might actually mean that your jokes were funny for once! Don't act like it's the first time I was ready early."

Cameron laughed, "I think it might be. New year, new Millie, huh? I like it. Let's go!" The two friends had been walking to school for years, and even in the worst weather, they attempted to keep the tradition going. It gave them an excellent chance to chat without having everyone else around.

"I can't believe that this is our last year of middle school," Millie said, "it's going to be weird next year when we start high school."

"I know, right?" Cameron replied. "But, I think most of us will stick together, so it shouldn't be too bad. It will be cool to have a bunch more kids around. Are you still skipping the state tryouts this year?" Cameron added, changing the topic.

"Yeah, I don't think I'm going to have time. Between schoolwork and our hockey trips away with the Lightning and Hurricanes, we'd miss most of the games anyway," Millie replied. "Actually, I *know* I won't have time."

"That's what Dad said too," Cameron said. "Plus, it will cost too much money for only half the games, and it wouldn't be fair on the other kids that miss out on the team if we weren't there for the full season."

"That's true. I hadn't thought of it that way. That would annoy me if I missed out on the team to some kids that didn't even play half the games," Millie replied.

Cameron and Millie spent the rest of their walk together talking about their upcoming hockey trips and laughing about the things they had gotten up to at the cottage over the summer.

"Wow," Georgia said, as they all sat down for lunch, "I forgot how much fun the first day of school is."

"Are you joking?" Rhys said, "I wouldn't even be awake yet if we were still on summer break."

"That's why your summer break felt so short," Hunter said laughing, "you slept through most of it!"

"Guys," Ashlyn said, getting everyone's attention as she and her sister walked up to the table, "Daylyn and I have some big news! Coach Phil and Janet are having a baby!" Then Daylyn blurted out, "we're going to be big sisters!"

All the kids crowded around the twins and congratulated them on the exciting news. There were lots of hugs from the girls, high fives, and even a few fist bumps from the boys.

"Why didn't you tell us at the park the other day?" Rhys asked, a little confused, "when we were all hanging out?"

"Well, we had to wait for our parents to tell everyone they needed to first. It took longer because we were away a lot over the summer, but now that they've told everyone they wanted, they said we could tell you guys!" Ashlyn said. "But it's been tough to keep it a secret, especially when we were hanging out together at the park."

"Yeah, I thought I was going to burst the other day!" Daylyn said laughing.

"Do you know if it's going to be a baby boy or a girl?" Sage asked.

"Yeah, are you going to have a baby brother or sister?" Rhys said.

"We don't know," Ashlyn replied, "they're going to wait so that it's a surprise."

"That's so cool," Cameron said, "sometimes I wish I had brothers and sisters, but I don't think I want to change diapers or share all my stuff,"

"Me either!" Rhys said, wrinkling up his nose and doing his best impression of someone

carrying toxic waste, which had all the kids laughing hysterically.

The kids spent the rest of their lunch break comparing baby sibling stories, some good, some bad, but there were a lot of laughs, and regardless of the stories, nothing would ruin the twins' excitement for the new baby entering their lives.

"How was the first day of school?" Millie's mom asked later that evening as she walked into Millie's room and sat down on her bed.

Millie had been in her room for several hours, busy transferring the individual class schedules she'd been given by all her teachers onto the large wall schedule she kept in her bedroom.

While Millie used to struggle a lot with organization and completing tasks, that had all changed. Once she had been diagnosed with ADHD, her parents and teachers organized additional help for her. The biggest thing she struggled with was staying on task and staying organized. Now, she was super organized at home and kept a large schedule to which she could add her class schedule, homework, tests, and assignments too.

"Good," Millie said, putting down the marker, "but better now I'm finished doing that. It's always a pain the first week, and it doesn't help that instead of giving us one schedule with all our classes, each teacher gives us an individual one."

"It looks like you're ready for anything," Millie's mom replied, looking at the detailed schedule on the wall. "I'm proud of you, by the way! Just in case I haven't mentioned it lately. Your dad is too."

"Thanks, Mom," Millie said, blushing. She never enjoyed getting compliments, but it still gave her a warm and fuzzy feeling. "It helps so much being able to see what I have coming up. No more stressing about assignments and missing deadlines because I can see them in advance and prepare."

"Okay, it's a great idea, and if it's working, then I say keep doing it," her mom said, getting up. "Dinner is ready downstairs, so come and relax and get something to eat. Your dad just got home, so I'm sure he wants to hear about your first day at school."

"Oh, he will," Millie said smiling, "I have some juicy news about Coach Phil and Janet."

"Let me guess," Millie's mom said, pretending to think really hard, "they're having a baby?"

"No fair!" Millie said laughing, "you already knew! There's no way you just guessed that out of thin air."

"Yes," her mom said, laughing and holding up her hands, "Janet texted me a few days ago, but she wanted the girls to be able to tell their friends first, so we had to keep it a secret."

"Boooo! You should have told me. I could have kept it a secret," Millie said, laughing as she got up, "you know you can trust me. Anyway, what's for dinner?"

"Steak and salad, and if we don't hurry up, the steak will get cold," her mom replied. "I know that I can trust you, but it wasn't my news to share."

THE GIRLS WERE still excited and buzzing about their upcoming European hockey trip. They had been invited to play in a hockey tournament by the Swedish girls' team, whom they had billeted in Dakota the year before during their international tournament.

However, it wasn't just a free trip away to play hockey. Just like the boys' upcoming hockey trip to Canada for the Great White North Tournament, the girls would be responsible for fundraising to cover some of the costs, such as plane tickets, accommodation, and meals.

Even though some of the girls had been invited to billet with the Swedish girls they had hosted in Dakota, the coaches had decided that, logistically, it would be just too difficult to organize. In addition, while some of the Swedish girls lived in the city of Stockholm itself, the majority lived spread out all over Sweden, and bussing and transportation could become a big problem.

Because most of the kids had been away over the summer and scattered all over the country, it had been hard to organize a group fundraiser, but all the kids had been selling raffle tickets around town whenever they were home. So that both teams didn't exhaust the same fundraising ideas, the coaches combined some events, like the big 50/50 raffle, and split up others. They didn't want the boys and girls doing the same fundraisers and tried to think outside the box for new fundraising ideas.

The 50/50 raffle was probably their biggest fundraiser. It would run the whole time, and the more tickets they sold, the bigger the prize would get and the more interested people would get. Both coaches hoped it alone would cover much of their costs, but it all depended on how many tickets the kids sold.

Now that they were back at school, with all the kids home from vacation, they were all ready to start their first group fundraising events. The girls had four months left until their trip, so it meant they had to buckle down if they wanted to cover the costs of their travels as much as possible. The boys' tournament was a few months later, so they had a bit more breathing room, but not enough that they could afford to take it easy either.

"Have we got all the signs set up, Millie?" Coach Phil asked, as he looked around the parking lot, "we don't want anyone driving past and missing out."

The girls' team had set up a carwash in the bowling alley's parking lot as their first big team event.

Because the bowling alley sponsored both hockey teams, they had agreed to double whatever the girls made. They had also blasted out the fundraising event on their social media pages to help them promote the carwash to a broader audience than just passing traffic.

The town of Dakota was a big hockey and sporting town. There were some famous hockey players who were born here and went on to play hockey professionally. While that meant there were often a lot of other teams doing fundraisers, it also meant plenty of people were willing to help support the kids with their fundraising efforts.

"Yes, Phil," Janet answered, rolling her eyes, and then winking at Millie, "some of us have been busy here for most of the morning setting up and not chatting to their friends at the coffee shop."

"Well, good, and here, I got you a decaf," Coach Phil said, handing over the coffee to his wife. Janet was the twins' mom and was married to Coach Phil. Because she was pregnant, she was trying to limit how much caffeine she drank.

"I guess that makes up for it, then," Janet laughed, "but a donut would have been nice too. This baby needs feeding," Janet said, as she rubbed her tummy.

"I'll be right back with a box of donuts," Coach Phil said laughing, "but I'm not sure it's the baby who needs the donuts or the mommy!"

"Don't you worry about who needs the donuts, mister," Janet said, shooing him on his way, "and be sure to bring back enough for the kids."

"Yes, please," Millie said smiling. It was cool the twins, Ashlyn and Daylyn, would have a brother or sister. It just sucked that Janet was due to have the baby in January, so she wouldn't be able to come on their hockey trip to Europe. Luckily, her mom had agreed to go instead of Janet. It was kind of reassuring knowing that her mom would be going with her, and she wouldn't have to fly by herself.

Considering summer was winding down, the weather was perfect for a carwash. It was a sunny Saturday morning, and the girls had set up early, which meant that their customers started showing up a little slower than expected, but within an hour or so, the carwash operation was in full swing!

Of course, it didn't hurt that next door to the bowling alley was one of the most popular coffee shops in town. It meant a lot of traffic passing the carwash as people went about their day and dropped by for a coffee or donut.

"Cameron! You missed the roof on that one!" Georgia shouted from where she was walking back and forth in her self-appointed role as car-wash supervisor.

"Yes, boss!" Cameron shouted back, throwing Georgia a mock salute, "I'll fix it!"

"Are you regretting getting out of the car yet?" Preston said quietly under his breath. The last thing that he wanted was Georgia hearing him. He wasn't scared of her but didn't fancy getting yelled at either.

"Yes," Cameron said laughing, "it looked like fun, throwing soap and bubbles around, but now it's looking a lot more like work."

Cameron had convinced his dad to come down and get a carwash, partially to help support the girls and somewhat to get out of him washing it later as part of his weekend chores. He'd seen Millie and all the girls having fun, so he'd decided to stay and help. However, he regretted his deci-sion now because instead of washing one car, he would be cleaning a bunch of cars half the day. To top it off, he had Georgia watching him and Pres-ton to ensure they did it correctly.

"Are you coming over to my place tonight?" Preston asked. Preston was having a few of the boys and girls over for pizza and a movie at his place later that night.

"Of course," Cameron said, looking down at his soaked clothes and wrinkled hands, laughing, "if I'm not too waterlogged!"

"Don't get caught having too much fun," Ashlyn said quietly with a wink, "otherwise dragon master will send us to the carwash jail."

"What was that?" Georgia shouted, "did someone call me?"

"No, Georgia," the three of them giggled, "we're all good."

"Oh, okay," Georgia replied, "you know you'll get more done with less chit-chat?"

"Yes, Georgia," they said, laughing even harder now.

"What's carwash jail?" Preston asked.

"I don't know," Ashlyn replied, "and I don't want to know, so just keep washing!"

The three of them started laughing again, and Cameron couldn't help but think how cute those two looked together. Preston and Ashlyn had started dating at the end of the school year, and whenever they thought no one was watching, they were always making googly lovey-dovey eyes at each other and smiling.

Cameron hadn't had a girlfriend since he'd broken up with Mia, and since she had moved away, they didn't talk much anymore. While he thought about it, Cameron made a mental note to message her later, see how she was doing, and fill her in on the gossip.

Cameron, Millie, Georgia, Rhys, Hunter, Khloe, Ashlyn, and Daylyn were all gathered around in the large cinema room at Preston's house later that night, thoroughly exhausted.

"I'm never doing another car wash for as long as I live," Rhys grumbled.

"But you were only there for an hour!" Georgia laughed, "most of us were there for the whole day so quit your grumbling."

"One hour was enough, and you're not the car-wash boss here," Rhys said, looking at his fingers that were still a little wrinkled, "hey, we're not doing a car wash fundraiser, are we?" he suddenly asked Cameron.

"No, we're not doing the same events as the girls so that people don't get sick of the same thing all the time. I think we're doing a meat sale, a bowl-a-thon, and a trip," Cameron said, thinking back to what Coach John had told him.

"Where is the trip to?" Rhys asked.

"The trip is to New York in a private jet, a night's accommodation, and tickets to a Broadway show," Preston answered, "my parents' business donated it."

"Oh, that's so awesome!" Khloe said, "I wish I were going on an all-expenses paid trip somewhere, even to a musical. What are we doing?" she asked, looking at the girls.

"We just did the carwash," Daylyn said, thinking, "and we still have a pasta night, oh, and the movie night!"

"Oh, what's the movie night?" Hunter asked, "that sounds fun. Can I help with that one?"

"Sure. We're hosting a movie night at the drive-in. We'll be selling tickets and also helping to run the food stand. I think it's two movies – a kid's movie, and a comedy."

"I'm definitely going to help with that one," Rhys said, with Hunter nodding in agreement, "who doesn't love going to the movies!"

"Pizza's here!" Preston's mom said as she walked into the theatre room carrying a stack of pizza boxes, "get'em while they're hot!"

"Is there a veggie pizza?" Ashlyn asked quietly.

"Of course, there is, dear," Preston's mom said laughing, "I wouldn't forget you. It's the one on the top."

"Oh, awesome! Thank you!" Ashlyn had recently had some digestive issues, and her doctor had suggested she try avoiding meat for a while. Her stomach issues had cleared up, and surprisingly, Ashlyn had enjoyed many of the vegetarian options, especially the veggie pizza. However, she still occasionally ate meat.

"You're welcome, honey," Preston's mom replied, "enjoy the pizza, kids!"

"Thanks!" they all chorused back, "we will."

The kids all tucked into the pizza while Preston started the movie. It was the boys' turn to pick the film, but instead of their typical action movie, they chose a comedy.

Not five minutes into the movie, a really funny scene had them all laughing hysterically, which caused Khloe to laugh so hard that she blew chunks of pizza all over the place. This had the entire group rolling on the floor, laughing and crying like lunatics.

Overall, the pizza and movie night was a big success, but most of the kids headed home fairly early as they were exhausted from washing cars all day. The boys had their bowl-a-thon coming up, and

Millie had agreed to come along with some other girls to help as the boys had offered to help with their movie night.

THE MOVIE NIGHT had gone perfectly, with the drive-in manager reporting back to the girls that it had been one of their biggest nights in recent times. Not only had they raised a lot of money for their hockey trip, but the manager had also donated a little extra to both teams for their upcoming tournaments and had committed to sponsoring both teams that season. Getting a new sponsor for the teams was always excellent, as it allowed them to enter more tournaments.

The girls' next big fundraising event was the pasta night, which was being hosted at the Italian Social Club. Because the girls were leaving for their trip to Europe before the boys went to Canada, they were trying to get most of their fundraising done early.

In the meantime, both teams had started off their regular hockey season with two wins. Like last season, they played Friday nights, and after home games, they were all having a pizza night, thanks to their sponsor at the bowling alley.

"It feels like we haven't had a weekend free for months!" Cameron said to Millie as they relaxed on Saturday morning.

"I know, right?" Millie said, sending another puck into the hockey net she had set up at the end of her driveway.

"It'll be too cold soon to do this for much longer," Cameron said, trying to flick a puck up onto the blade of his stick before shooting it unsuccessfully into the net, "have to get the basement net set up."

"I miss summer already," Millie said, sighing, "and you still haven't worked out that trick shot, huh?" Then, as she finished speaking, she did the exact same thing that Cameron had been trying to do and sent the puck flying into the top right corner.

"Whatever!" Cameron said, shaking his head. For some reason, Millie had always been a little better at the trick shots they watched online, picking them up faster than him every time. Of course, he'd get it in the end, but until then, he'd have to deal with that silly smirk plastered all over her face.

"It's okay, Cam," Millie said laughing, "we both know who's better at the trick shots."

"Show me one more time," Cameron said, after he messed it up again for about the fiftieth time in a row, "I'll get it this time."

"Please," Millie said sweetly.

Cameron looked at the sky, hoping a fiery meteor would appear before hurtling down and landing on him. "Please, can you show me how you're doing the trick again?" He replied through gritted teeth, as politely as his patience allowed him in the current situation.

"That's better," Millie said, smiling innocently, knowing full well that she was driving him crazy, "now you want to lay the front of the blade down flat on the puck, as close to the heel of the ticks as possible, leaving just a tiny bit of blade hanging off the back like this," Millie said, demonstrating with her stick.

"Like this?" Cameron said, copying her.

"Yep. If you push on the puck, you should be able to rock it back and forth," Millie said, show-ing him.

"Oh, yeah," Cameron said, moving the puck back and forth like Millie had done. "What's next?"

"Now," Millie said, continuing, "just push down and backward on the puck as you bring the stick up to your waist," she said, demonstrating, "and if you want to take it to the full shot, you just push through and take the shot. You can pick it up high to do tricks or just a few inches to take the shot."

Cameron watched as Millie did the trick and then did it successfully a few times himself, just practicing picking up the puck and dropping it again until he got comfortable enough to do the whole trick with the shot, sending the puck sailing into the net.

"There you go," Millie said, slowly clapping, "now you got it, buddy!"

The two continued to practice taking shots for another hour until they got bored before going inside to make some lunch and watch a movie.

"That bowling night was epic!" Rhys said to the kids as they sat together eating their lunch at school on Monday. "We should do that again!"

"I have to admit," Hunter added, I thought I would be getting sick of bowling because we're doing it every other Friday, but the way we set it up with the music and the switching lanes was hilarious."

"Not for me!" Millie said, shaking her head, "I got Cameron's lane." Cameron wasn't bad at bowling, but he'd been messing around with the other boys that night, and their team score wasn't great. Millie was super competitive and had drawn the short straw when they had drawn out two teams to swap lanes. First, she had gone from second place to last place, and then Cameron's team had gone on to win the tournament.

"Aww, Millie," Cameron said laughing, "no hard feelings, but thanks for the win!"

"Yeah, we got a bunch of cool stuff," Rhys added, before going on to list all the prizes they had won.

"Yeah, yeah. Okay, I have to go," Millie said, standing up, "I have a meeting with my tutor next period. Bye!"

"How was school, Millie?" her mom asked when she got home later that day. "How did that meeting go?" Millie had regular meetings with her tutor to ensure she wasn't getting behind in her classes.

"It was good, but she's going to add in some afternoon sessions. Between the fundraising stuff, hockey games, and the fact that I'll be losing time when I go away, she thought it would be a good idea so I don't get behind," Millie said.

"Are you struggling a bit?" Millie's mom asked, concerned, "are you taking on too much?"

"Well," Millie began, "I'm all up to date, but I feel like the last two weeks I've had to really push myself not to fall behind. The tutor said if I feel that I'm losing control, it's better to get it sorted out before it gets worse."

"That's true," her mom said. "I'm glad you've got it under control. She's a smart lady, your tutor. Are you getting hungry?"

"Yeah," Millie said, noticing the time. "What's for dinner anyway?"

"Dad's making burgers with those bacon-wrapped onion rings he watched on a video or something," her mom replied, shaking her head. Millie laughed. Her dad was always watching those weird food cooking videos online and then making the rest of them eat them. Sometimes it felt like they were prisoners or contestants on one of those strange reality shows on TV.

"Well, I just hope that they end up better than the air-fried peanut butter and jelly sandwich things he forced us to eat the other day," Mille said, pretending to vomit.

"They better for his sake," her mom said, "I'm not in the mood to play around with his strange recipes tonight!"

Lying in bed later that night, Millie sent Cameron a photo of the bacon-wrapped onion rings her dad had made for dinner.

He texted straight back with a drooling emoji followed by bacon, which made Millie laugh. He then asked what they were, so she explained the whole thing to him.

Cameron also filled her in on his conversation with Mia and caught her up on the gossip, which reminded Millie that she also needed to text Mia. So, she sent Mia a quick text before saying good-night to Cameron and putting her phone on the charger. The last thing he texted back was a question about leftovers for breakfast, which made her laugh.

Trust Cameron to want to eat bacon-wrapped deep-fried onion rings for breakfast. The boys were gross sometimes, and if any of them stopped playing sports, they would probably end up the size of a house.

"OKAY, GIRLS," MR. Rossi began, "we have a packed house tonight! You've done an excellent job of selling out the restaurant, but unfortunately for you, that means we're all going to be very busy!"

"That's great, Mr. Rossi," Khloe said, "time flies when you're busy!"

"Good, good. Now, let's go through what you'll be doing tonight. Because this is a special event, we have set up the projector at the front of the restaurant to play the hockey game. Then, at half-time, we'll do the silent auction. I'll need you girls to help greet and seat the guests, take orders, and deliver food to the tables. I also need some people to help in the kitchen. So, anyone who wants to help in the kitchen, raise your hand!"

Khloe, Sage, Ashlyn, Daylyn, and two juniors, Kiera and Maddie, volunteered to go and help in the kitchen. Millie, Georgia, Violet, and Lola all volunteered to help with the front of the restaurant and table waiting.

The girls didn't have to wait long for the first guests to start arriving. The front restaurant girls had been busy learning how to take orders, and the seating layout of the tables, so they could seat guests and explain the menu as they arrived. The servers had shown them around the restaurant and would be there to jump in if they needed any help.

To make the evening a little easier, they would run a set menu with a vegetarian, chicken, and beef option, a salad, a starter, and dessert.

In the kitchen, the girls helped with plating up, cleaning dishes, and assisting the chefs with whatever tasks they needed. Because the kitchen was small, it was a little crowded and hot, but so far, they were all having fun with music playing and all the girls were learning how a restaurant kitchen runs.

"It's so hot in here!" Khloe said, wiping another bead of sweat from her forehead.

"I know, right?" Ashlyn said, from where she was cracking eggs into a large bowl for the dessert station, "I never knew how hot kitchens were." For all the girls, it was their first time in a real kitchen. The kitchen they used at school for their cooking class was a lot bigger, with more room, and it never got this hot, even in the middle of summer.

"Our kitchen at home is nothing like this," Kiera said, "my dad barely looks like he breaks a sweat when he's making our dinner."

"Commercial kitchens are always hot," one of the chefs added with a chuckle, overhearing the girls' conversation, "you should come and see what it's like in the middle of summer!"

"I hate to imagine how hot it is then," Maddie sighed. "Y'all must melt!"

"You get used to it," another chef added, "and this kitchen isn't nearly as hot as some kitchens I've worked in over the years. You girls are doing a great job, by the way. A lot of kids would have given up already."

"It's because we're hockey players and Hurricanes," Daylyn said proudly, "we don't give up!"

"I always wanted to be a chef," Sage added, "and this hasn't changed my mind one bit."

"It's a great job," one of the chefs said, with a wink, "and we're always looking for kitchen hands to help with prep and cleaning. It's a great way to learn on the job and how I got my start. So, when you ladies are looking for jobs next year, I'd be happy to put in a good word for you with Mr. Rossi. You've been great so far."

Both Khloe and Sage had silly grins plastered all over their faces. Both girls had a passion for food

and cooking, and getting any sort of job in the restaurant industry had always been a dream for them.

"Thanks, Chef!" they both chorused back, sharing a quick excited look before quickly getting on with their tasks.

Meanwhile, at the front of the restaurant, all the guests were seated, but not without some confusion. Millie and Georgia had tried to seat two families at the same table, and Lola had taken one group on two laps of the restaurant before she'd managed to find the correct table. However, after the initial rush of everyone arriving, the girls had been moving from table to table, making small talk, and walking all the guests through the menu.

Before they knew it, it was half-time in the hockey match, and the restaurant owner, Mr. Rossi, had taken over the announcing role to call out the winners of the silent auction. Throughout appetizers and seating, guests had been writing down their bids for a number of prizes, which were on tables near the front of the restaurant. Many local businesses and sponsors had donated prizes for the event.

It was clear that Mr. Rossi wasn't new to announcing and had the entire restaurant cheering and laughing as he announced the winners. He also took a moment to thank not only the guests and donors of prizes but also the girls for their hard work. Then, with the auction prizes given out, it was time for the main course to be served.

"You know what," Georgia said to Millie as the pair delivered main courses to the last of their assigned tables, "waitressing is hard work!"

"They always look so happy and cheerful," Millie added, "but being on your feet all night is hard work. No wonder they appreciate tips!"

"I think I have a blister," Sage said, rubbing her boot. "Yes, I definitely have a blister."

"Please," Violet said, leaning against the pass counter where the meals came out from the kitchen, "my blisters have blisters, and I'm so hungry!"

"We made extra for after service," Khloe said, leaning through from the kitchen, "we're all going to have a sit-down dinner with the chefs and other staff when the guests leave."

"Wow!" Millie said, "that's so cool."

"You girls earned it," Mr. Rossi said, as he walked through, "this has been one of the best events like this I've hosted. We have about ten minutes if you want to take turns having a break and a drink, then we'll start clearing the main courses, get dessert out, and it'll be almost closing time."

It may have felt like they were in the restaurant for a day and a night, but soon the last of the guests had left for the evening, and the girls had an opportunity for a much-needed rest before they began cleaning up. Once the front of the restaurant team had finished, they moved to the back to the rest of the girls and the chefs cleaning up and preparing the traditional family dinner.

It wasn't long before everyone found themselves sitting down at one of the long tables at the back of the restaurant with a long line of different dishes spread out on the table in front of them.

"Girls, I just want to say that it was a pleasure hosting this event for you, and I wish you all the best on your European trip! I wish I was going with you. I could slip over to Italy to visit with friends and family. Now, all of you did great tonight. It was smooth sailing all night. So, sit down and enjoy a family dinner with us. We do this after service every night. It's good to relax and enjoy some nice food, and the chefs are allowed to prepare new meals that they've been trying," Mr. Rossi said as he sat down.

"Mr. Rossi," Millie began, "on behalf of all of us Hurricanes, we would like to thank you for your support and thank you for the opportunity. I think I'm speaking for all of us when I say that I never truly knew how hard it is working in a restaurant and how hard everyone works to prepare and serve meals to customers. Thanks for the opportunity!"

This response got a round of applause from all the chefs, wait staff, the girls, and Mr. Rossi.

"Cheers, Millie," Mr. Rossi said, raising his glass, "and in honor of Italy, *Salute!*"

The next morning there was a big conversation in the girls' group chat about their night spent at the restaurant. A few of them, particularly Sage and Khloe, had loved working in the kitchen and were already planning out their careers.

While Millie had enjoyed the night and wouldn't mind getting a job in a restaurant when she was old enough to work, she didn't have any aspirations of becoming a chef. Now, as she thought about it, she hadn't really thought about what she wanted to do when she was older. It was something she'd need to remember to speak to her tutor or counselor about the next time they had a meeting.

She still had a lot of time to think about careers, but it never hurt to have a goal to work towards.

The Italian night was the last of the girls' big fundraisers, except for the 50/50 raffle, which they were sharing with the boys. After that, they didn't have any events left to organize. They still had a few small things they were doing, but they would have a meeting soon to discuss how much money they had raised and what the parents would need to cover.

THE BOYS HAD started selling tickets to their meat raffle, with a local butcher donating three large meat trays valued at $300, $200, and $100. The tickets were selling well around town, but they probably should have started their meat raffle at the start of summer when everyone was barbequing.

Regardless, every little bit would help them fundraise for their trip to Canada in January next year. On Friday night, they were drawing their 50/50 raffle after their hockey match and judging by the number of tickets they had sold, it was going to be a huge prize.

"Could this week drag by any slower?" Georgia grumbled at lunch, "I mean, it's Thursday already, but I want to go to Sweden already!"

"We have the game tomorrow night and the 50/50 raffle draw," Lola said, "then I think we have a team meeting with our parents on Saturday afternoon about the Europe trip."

"Oh, that's right," Millie said, "Mom reminded me about it last night after dinner."

"What's the meeting about, Millie?" Cameron asked.

"I think they'll have the total of what we fund-raised, and then they'll be able to see how much the parents get reimbursed," Millie replied.

"Reimbursed?" Rhys asked, confused, "what are they getting reimbursed for?"

"Our parents already paid for the insurance, accommodation, flights, meals, and things like that so that we could get everything booked early," Georgia explained, "but the fundraising money will go back to them to help cover the costs."

"Oh, cool," Hunter said, nodding, "I guess that's how ours will work as well?"

"Yep," Cameron said, "so the more we raise, the less our parents will need to pay."

The kids spent the rest of lunch comparing their fundraising efforts before the bell rang.

"Yep, yep!" Millie shouted, banging the blade of her stick against the ice, signaling that she was open to Georgia, who was skating hard up the ice. Georgia didn't hesitate, flicking the puck up the ice toward where Millie had broken away from the girl covering her.

Millie took the puck cleanly, pushing hard towards the goalie who was shimmying back and forth in her crease, not sure where the shot was going, but knowing that it was coming in hot any second. Millie wound up as if she was taking a big slap shot, but at the last second, pulled the shot and flicked it low, right into the five-hole between the goalie's legs.

Goal! That quick goal by Millie took the girls to a 3–1 lead with four minutes left in the final period.

"Great shot, Millie," Coach Phil said, giving her a fist bump as she skated up to the bench.

"Thanks, Coach," Millie replied, puffing a bit. She'd been on the ice a lot this game, and it was starting to show.

"You and Georgia are done for the rest of the game," Coach Phil said, "I'll give some of the juniors a run out on the ice. Great job!"

So far this season, this would be their fourth win in a row, and none of the other teams had been super challenging. However, they had some

tough games coming up when they got back from their trip to Sweden.

On the other rink, the boys weren't having nearly as easy a time as the girls. Cameron had taken a large hit in the first period, colliding with Rhys and a player from the other team before sliding into the boards. He was okay but had hurt his knee during the fall, so he was sitting out the rest of the game.

Unfortunately, Rhys was also pretty banged up. Currently, the score was tied 1–1, with only about three minutes left in the last period.

"I think I can skate, Coach," Cameron said, hating the fact that he had sat on the bench for most of the game while his team hadn't managed to get another score on the board.

"No," Coach John, the Lightning coach, replied, "rest your knee. There's no need to risk you getting even more hurt for a mid-season game. I know it's not ideal, but safety first, buddy. I'll call a time-out, and we'll see if we can get it done."

This wasn't the answer Cameron was looking for, but now it was up to the kids out on the ice, including the two juniors Chase and Reid, to try and break the tie.

"They're weak on their left side," Cameron said to Chase during the quick 30-second time-out, "go up their left side, drag the defender from the right, then pass back to Reid."

"Okay, no worries, I'll do my best," Chase replied, panting and puffing, visibly out of breath after taking so many back-to-back shifts, before heading onto the ice to get back into position.

Chase took the puck and waited for the rest of the team to get into position before pushing up the ice. Then, he faked out the two forwards that came rushing down the ice towards him, passing the puck off to Reid at the last second before cutting through both players.

Reid didn't hold the puck long, passing across the ice to Chase, who was pushing up the left side, drawing the two defenders towards him. Chase skated around the first defender and positioned himself as if he was going to do the same again, but instead passed off the puck to Reid, who'd kept pace in the center.

The goalie focused on Chase and tried desperately to reposition himself to the new threat on the right side, but his reaction speed was just a little bit off, with Chase driving the puck home into the top right corner of the net!

Goal! With only thirty seconds left on the clock, the boys had taken the score to 2–1 in their favor.

Now, they just had to hang on for thirty seconds, and the win would be theirs.

The final thirty seconds of the game were anti-climactic, with the Lightning defenders doing an awesome job killing the puck and keeping it well away from Logan's net. The boys took the win, and it was a great job for the juniors who stepped up.

"I can't believe that the 50/50 raffle prize money was $5,955!" Millie said to Georgia and some of the other girls as they sat waiting for Coach Phil, Janet, and Millie's mom to tally up their final fundraising amount.

"That means we get $5,955?" Khloe asked.

"No," Georgia replied, "we have to split it with the boys. Half each."

"Oh yeah," Khloe said laughing, "I forgot about the stinky boys getting half. Either way, it's a great result. Can't wait to find out how much we made in total."

Just then, Coach Phil, Janet, and Millie's mom walked back into the room.

"Thank you all for coming," Coach Phil started, "I won't waste too much of your time. The grand total of fundraising was $7,153." The figure got a round of applause and pats on the back from the parents and kids gathered in the room.

"When we take that off the total amount paid for the trip, it means you're all going to get a bit over one-third of your money back. I really have to say, the girls and parents, you have all done an amazing job. I'll put the exact amounts in an email, and if you can let me know if you want a check or bank deposit, I'll make sure that goes through on Monday or Tuesday."

"Yes, great job, everyone!" Janet said, clapping, her bump getting very noticeable now, "I just wish I was going with y'all." Janet was due to have her baby in early January, so it meant she couldn't fly.

"In the interests of keeping this short and sweet, I'll let you all get back to your Saturday afternoons. Now, if anyone has any questions," Coach Phil stopped, "I'll hang back and try to answer them. Otherwise, have a great weekend!"

Most of the parents and kids stood up and said their goodbyes before heading for the exit. It had been a massive fundraising effort from both the parents and the girls. They were all looking forward to a few days of relaxation without any fundraising before leaving for their trip.

"TOMORROW IS THE big day, huh?" Rhys asked Georgia and Millie as they played video games in Millie's basement.

"Yeah," Millie replied, "not going to lie, I'm a little nervous."

"Same," Georgia replied, "this will be the longest trip I've ever been on."

"You'll be fine," Rhys said, waving away their concerns, "think about us stuck here with nothing to do while you're gone for a month on a European vacation!"

"Firstly, it's a week," Millie said, rolling her eyes, "and secondly, it's not all vacation. We're going for a hockey tournament."

"Thirdly," Georgia said, chiming in, "we'll be in the same position when you all go to Canada next year."

"They've got you there, buddy," Cameron said, throwing the controller over to Rhys, "can't argue with their logic."

The four of them had been as thick as thieves lately, and it would be strange for all of them to be going on separate trips, but it would become more common. Playing on different teams, participating in other tournaments, and even separate leagues became more common as the kids got older.

"Apart from being nervous about being so far from home," Cameron asked, "are you both excited about the trip?"

"For sure," Millie replied, "My mom's coming with us as a team assistant and chaperone, so I'm not too nervous, but I can understand why the others are."

"Yeah, Mom and Dad have been watching too many documentaries on television," Georgia said, shaking her head, "you would think I was going to spend a week with pirates or something."

The boys laughed. They knew they would be going through the same experience themselves soon enough, but to a lesser extent because their trip was only to Canada, not Europe.

"What time is the flight?" Rhys asked, losing again to the big boss and passing the controller to Georgia.

"Early," Georgia said, trying to concentrate on the game, "too early."

"It wouldn't matter if the flight were in the afternoon," Cameron said laughing, "it would still be too early for you, Georgia!"

"She's not a morning person," Millie said, agreeing, "but the flight is pretty early. It leaves at nine, so we need to be at the airport by six a.m."

"See?" Georgia said, "too early!"

"That's way too early for me," Rhys agreed, "luckily, we're only going to Canada and won't have to leave in the middle of the night." Millie just shook her head. Georgia and Rhys were the two laziest of her friends and often slept in well into the day.

The four friends spent the rest of the afternoon playing video games and chatting, but it was soon time for Millie and Georgia to finish packing and get ready.

"Are you girls all packed?" Millie's dad said as they finished clearing the dishes away after dinner.

"We certainly are," Millie's mom replied. "Are you ready to enjoy your week alone?"

"Oh, it's going to be hard to survive all week alone," Millie's dad said dramatically, "I'm not sure how I'm going to get through the week."

"Sure thing, funny guy," Millie's mom said, swatting him on the arm, "just don't go eating junk food all week. You know how to cook!"

"Yeah, Dad," Millie said, teasing him, "this isn't a pizza for dinner every night vacation for you!"

"I'll have you both know that I don't plan on eating pizza every night," her dad said laughing, "but it's definitely going to happen at least once while you're gone!"

The three of them spent the rest of the evening going through their itinerary and double-checking their passports and bags before it was time for bed.

Millie was trying to go to sleep but found it hard. She had a million thoughts running through her head, and even though she knew she had to be up early, she just couldn't fall asleep.

It felt like hours and hours, but it wasn't really before Millie eventually drifted off to sleep, listening to music playing softly in the background.

Tomorrow was going to be a big day!

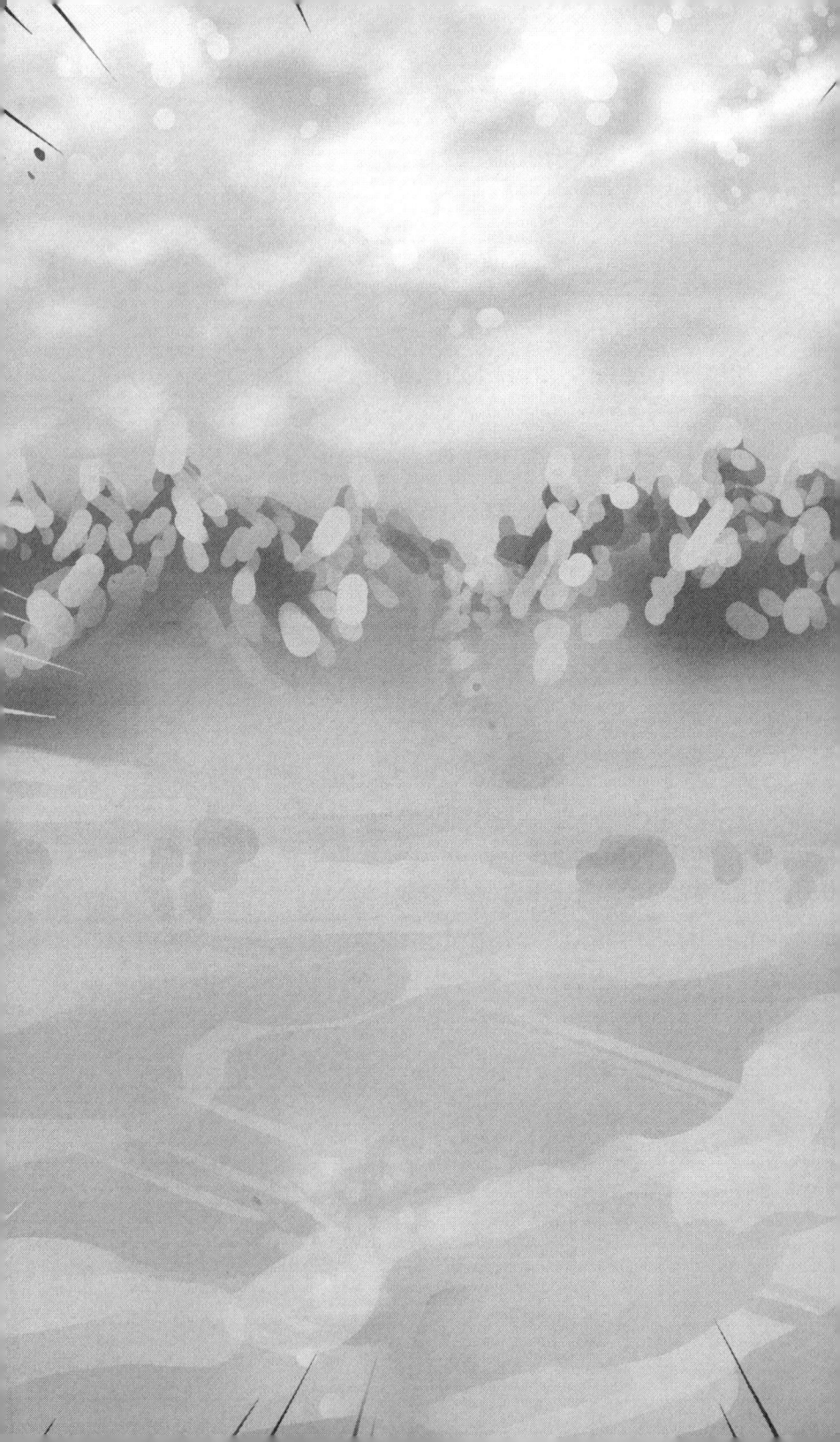

"RIGHT, IS EVERYONE here?" Coach Phil said, doing a quick head count and checking it off against a list he had brought along.

The group of kids and parents were in the airport departures area doing a final round of goodbyes before they went through security.

"Okay," Coach Phil said, finished with the list, "we're all here. Now, say your final goodbyes because once I give out the tickets, we'll all check in and then go through security. Make sure you have your passport ready."

This announcement led to a rush of final goodbyes before the girls lined up at the security checkpoint. You needed a ticket to get through security, and once through the checkpoint, you couldn't walk back out.

Coach Phil was giving Janet a final goodbye hug.

"She looks like she's about to pop!" Georgia said to the twins.

"We were joking around last night about it," Ashlyn said, giggling. "Daylyn said she looks like an overripe tomato!"

"It didn't go over well," Daylyn said, shaking her head with a grin, "as you'd expect."

The girls slowly filtered through the first checkpoint, where they had to show their passports and tickets before lining up at the security scanning station. Then, each of them had to take off their shoes, empty their pockets, and place their bags on the conveyor belt. They'd all been given a long list of what not to put in their bags, except for one of the juniors, Maize, who had packed a big bottle of shampoo which was confiscated after another lecture from security about what not to pack in carry-on bags.

The next step was to clear customs, which was busy and took almost thirty minutes before all the girls had made their way through, but there were no issues, and they were finally through and into the lounge area.

"Okay, girls," Millie's mom said, gathering them all together, "if you look at your boarding pass, it says which gate we're all leaving from and when we're boarding. Now, if you look at the board, it also says the same thing. We're all going to walk up to the gate," she stopped speaking to check her watch, "and we have an hour until the flight leaves. So you're allowed to walk around a little, but don't go too far from the gate and ensure you're back at least ten minutes before that boarding time."

A lot of the juniors decided to find somewhere comfortable to sit down, a little nervous about exploring too far, but along with the other seniors on the team, Millie, Georgia, and Khloe went for a walk around the airport.

"I never thought about the airport being this big inside," Khloe said to the other girls, "it's like a small city!" The girls had walked through the food court area, past all the gift shops, and even found a part of the airport that was full of massage chairs.

"Yeah," Georgia added, "I was so little the last time I flew anywhere that I can barely remember. Do you guys have a book to read and snacks?"

"Not yet," Millie said, "I was waiting until after we went through security before I grabbed anything. I do have my phone with some movies downloaded for the flight, though."

"Okay, let's go back and go into that big shop we passed earlier and grab everything, so it's done before boarding starts," Khloe said, looking at her watch, "we have about fifteen minutes until boarding time."

The three girls finished their shopping before the flight, then headed back to join the rest of the girls in the gate area until boarding started.

"See, taking off wasn't that bad," Millie's mom said to Georgia and Millie, "nothing to worry about."

Millie, her mom, and Georgia were all sitting next to each other on the flight. Luckily, the flight attendants had let all the girls board first, after the first-class passengers, which meant they had plenty of time to get comfortable and find their seats. Once they were settled, the rest of the flight had boarded, and it wasn't long before they found themselves in the air and on the way to Europe.

After the welcome announcement by the captain, the seatbelt light was switched off, and the girls were free to move around the cabin and talk to one another. It didn't take long for everyone to get over the initial excitement and settle into the routine of the plane ride.

The only girl on the team who had been upset when the plane took off was Violet. She had been nervous about the flight from the start, especially the take-off and landing, so Coach Phil had her sit next to him for take-off, and the stewardess had taken some time to explain the process and how there was nothing to worry about.

"Hi, we're raising money for our hockey tournament and a trip to Canada next year. Would you be interested in buying a ticket in our meat raffle?" Rhys said when the lady opened the door, quickly going through the major prizes and how much the tickets were.

"Sure, boys," the lady said smiling, "give me a second. I'll go and grab my purse."

"Thank you, ma'am," Rhys said with a large smile, "see? Now next house, you just do the same."

"I don't know how you're so good at this," Cameron said, shaking his head, "I don't know if it's just dumb luck or you're a natural salesperson." The two boys had been walking around all morning selling tickets for their last fundraiser. Rhys had sold tickets at almost every house he'd done, but for some reason, Cameron wasn't having as much luck.

"There you go," the lady said, handing over a ten-dollar bill, "I'll take two tickets, please."

As Rhys took down her name, address, and phone number, Cameron ran through the speech a few times in his head before they had to knock on the next door.

"Thanks," both boys chorused before walking down the driveway and along the path to the next house.

"You have to be confident," Rhys said, "and less nervous. People think you're up to no good when you're all jittery and nervous and ruining the speech."

Cameron took a deep breath and knocked confidently on the door. When the man opened, Cameron introduced himself and Rhys, then went into the sales speech they'd been working on.

"Umm," the man hesitated, "sure. Let me check my wallet but it sounds good. You can never have too much meat."

"See," Rhys said, punching Cameron on the arm, "you just have to be more confident."

The man returned and bought three tickets.

"Thanks!" both boys said before setting off for the next street on the list. Each of the boys had been paired up and given a list of roads to do. This way, the whole team wouldn't be doing the same area and annoying people. They had a bit of a walk to the next street, and Rhys pulled out his phone to check the flight app.

"Okay, flight update," Rhys said, checking the app, "the girls are now about this far out over the Atlantic Ocean," he said, showing Cameron the little plane flying along its path toward Sweden.

"That app is cool," Cameron said, "is it free?"

"Yep," Rhys replied, "just download the app when you get back home to the Wi-Fi."

"Does it say how long until they arrive?" Cameron asked, "they took off about an hour ago."

"Yeah," Rhys said, clicking on the plane icon, "it says they took off about one hour and twenty-two minutes ago and should arrive in eight hours, thirty minutes ahead of schedule."

"That's cool," Cameron replied, "but that's such a long time to spend sitting on a plane."

"Yea, I'm not sure I could do it," Rhys added, "I'd go loopy. But, hey, here's the next street on the list. Is it my turn or your turn?"

"My turn," Cameron answered, "let me work my magic again."

Rhys laughed, "okay, salesman of the year. Let's see how you go and if you can get two in a row!"

"How's your book, Millie?" her mom asked, "any good?"

"Yeah, it is," Millie said, sliding a bookmark into place and closing the book, "but I can't wait to get off the plane. I'm super fidgety."

"Same," Georgia added, "will it be daytime or nighttime when we arrive?"

"Umm," Millie's mom looked at her notes, "It'll be nighttime or evening, so not too bad. By the time we clear customs and get out of the airport, it'll be late, though, so probably straight to bed once we get to the hotel."

Their flight so far had been entirely uneventful. All the girls had been given lunch pretty soon after taking off, then dinner not long ago. The captain had announced that they'd be arriving in about thirty minutes and to get settled for landing. There had been a little minor turbulence for about five minutes, and they had to put their seatbelts back on, but apart from that, it had been a very smooth flight.

After a few minutes, the captain announced that everyone had to take their seats and prepare for landing. He also told them that if they looked out their windows on either side of the plane, they could see the city's lights.

Millie looked past Georgia to the millions of twinkling lights below them. "It looks so big!" After spending almost eight hours flying over nothing, it was refreshing to see the ground below.

"There are so many lights down there!" Georgia said, looking out the window next to Millie, "it must be so huge!"

The plane started to descend and slow down, and then they all heard loud clunks of the wheels dropping down and the landing gear sliding into place.

As the plane slowed, the girls could start to see more and more details, and then they were gliding to the runway, with the airport buildings rushing past them. Then, with a loud screech, the plane wheels hit the tarmac, and the captain started braking before the announcement system came to life.

"Ladies and gentlemen, welcome to Stockholm, Sweden! And a special good luck to the girls of the Dakota Hurricanes in their hockey tournament." The last part got a loud cheer from the girls and clapping from some of the other passengers around them, "enjoy your time in Sweden, and thanks for flying with us. We hope to see you again in the air!"

The girls had arrived! They were in Sweden.

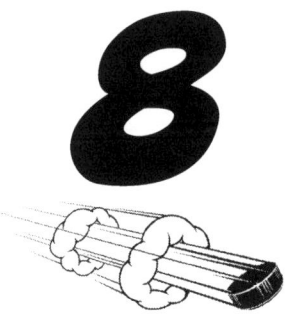

"What is the purpose of your visit to Sweden?" the customs agent asked Millie and her mom as they both stepped up for their turn at the customs desk.

"A hockey tournament," Millie's mom answered, handing over their passports, "we're traveling together with the rest of the team."

All the girls had been placed in the same customs line to make it easier for the customs agent and the girls. In addition, it meant that they wouldn't have to explain why they were traveling to Stockholm in such detail repeatedly.

Whenever you traveled internationally, even to countries close to the United States, like Canada, you had to go through customs when you arrived. At customs, they usually checked your passport and visa and asked you questions about why you were visiting, what you were doing, and how long you would be there.

"Ah yes," the customs agent replied smiling, "I see. Of course. Enjoy your visit to Sweden, and good luck in your hockey tournament," she said, stamping their passports and handing them back before signaling the next girl in line to step up.

"Thank you," Millie and her mom replied before walking through the gate and waiting at the end of the hall. Coach Phil and Millie's mom had split up, with Millie's mom going through first and Coach Phil bringing up the rear. The coaches had already told the girls where to meet after customs in case anyone got separated.

The group of girls breezed through customs without problems, but they hadn't expected any. The next step would be to head down to the luggage area, pick up their suitcases, and then they would be on the bus to the hotel.

The private shuttle bus taking them to the hotel was waiting outside the baggage carousel area. The driver had walked into the terminal holding a small sign with '*Dakota Hurricanes*' printed neatly on it. Rather than rely on the free hotel shuttles, Coach Phil and Millie's mom had booked a private shuttle to ensure that all the girls could ride together and they wouldn't need to separate the group at all.

Even though it was late, the girls were full of energy and were busy connecting to Wi-Fi, taking selfies, and sending messages to their parents to let them know they'd all arrived safely in Sweden.

"Once you see your suitcase and your hockey bag come along, grab it, and then head over to the bus driver and wait there for the rest of the team," Coach Phil said, "and make sure you don't block the exit or go wandering off. Once we get all the bags, we'll be onto the bus and straight to the hotel. I'll be grabbing any hockey bags I see and piling them up next to me, so if you see yours, come grab it."

Before they left, Millie's mom had set up a group chat for all the parents to keep everyone updated. Unfortunately, not all the girls were as quick to send a message, and this way, no one would be missing an update. So, she sent a quick photo of all the girls waiting near the driver with their suitcases, letting them know they had arrived safely, and would soon be heading to the hotel to check in.

Surprisingly, every single bag made it from Dakota to Stockholm without issue. Millie's hockey bag had a small rip where it had been caught in some machinery along the way, but there were no lost or missing bags to deal with.

"How far is the hotel?" Georgia asked Millie's mom as they sat down on the bus, "hours or minutes?"

"About ten minutes, according to the itinerary the shuttle company sent us," Millie's mom replied, "you'll be able to shower, relax, grab something to eat, and call home."

"Ah, okay," Georgia replied, "I can't wait to get into my pajamas."

"Me either," Millie replied, "traveling is fun but exhausting!"

As the bus traveled along the nighttime streets of Stockholm, the girls were all surprised at just how much activity there was. People were still shopping, eating in restaurants, drinking coffee, and looking around at the city's lights.

It was so much busier than Dakota and made their town feel so much smaller.

"Look! People are skating!" Khloe shouted from the front of the bus, causing all the girls to rush to the window to look at where a group of people were skating on a large public ice rink next to a big market area.

"Oh, that's so cool!" the girls shouted, "will we be able to skate here too?"

"Is our hotel close by?" Sage asked Coach Phil.

"Hmm," Coach Phil thought, "I think we have free time in the schedule to look around the city, so I don't see why we wouldn't be able to squeeze in a quick skate."

This announcement by Coach Phil had all the girls cheering.

Considering that we've just flown halfway around the world, they don't look or sound tired at all, Millie's mom thought, laughing. But, of course, that would all change once they got settled into their room and into pajamas!

"Why am I getting tired so fast?" Georgia said, yawning and stretching out on the bed.

The girls had all managed to get checked into their suites pretty quickly once they had arrived at the hotel.

It would be four girls in a room, with the coaches and Millie's mom getting their own room.

Millie, Georgia, Khloe, and Sage were all rooming together, with Georgia and Millie sharing one room and Khloe and Sage in the other room. Each suite had two bedrooms, a lounge area, and a bathroom.

"Don't forget we've pretty much been up all day and half the night now," Sage replied, "it's a long day. I'm ready for bed."

All the girls had showered, changed, and unpacked and were lying or sitting on the couches while they texted and called their parents to let them know they had arrived and were heading to bed.

With a round of goodnights, the girls all headed for their beds. Millie and Georgia were so tired that they didn't even chat, which was a first for them. Usually, if they were sleeping over, there would be several hours of talk about school, hockey, and boys before they drifted off to sleep. However, tonight it had been a quick goodnight, earbuds in, and straight to sleep for both girls.

Just before she put her phone down for the night, Millie remembered to send Cameron a quick text message, and within minutes she found herself drifting off to sleep.

"I DIDN'T REALIZE that I would be this hungry," Millie said to her mom as she finished off her second plate of fruit and pancakes.

"It's the time zone change, mixed in with the start of a little jetlag, airplane food, not drinking enough water, and just being awake so much yesterday, I imagine."

"True," Millie said, thinking for a minute, "you don't notice how much being in a hotel and airplane dehydrates you. How did you sleep?"

"Like a zombie," her mom replied, "your dad wasn't here to keep me up all night with his snoring either!"

Millie started laughing so hard that a big piece of half-chewed watermelon fell out of her mouth and into her lap before bouncing onto the floor under the table, causing her mom to laugh and shake her head. Who knows what the other people enjoying breakfast in the large dining room must have thought? Probably that they were both a little strange, but neither Millie nor her mom cared. They were having too much fun.

"Good morning, ladies," Georgia said, swinging herself into an empty seat next to Millie and her mom, "I'm starving!"

"That's funny. We were just talking about that before you got here," Millie's mom said, "are you both excited about touring around the city today and seeing more of Stockholm?"

"Of course," Georgia replied, shoveling a spoon-ful full of hot scrambled eggs into her mouth, "we were just talking about it upstairs in our room, and by the way, Millie, you won't be impressed."

"Why not?" Millie said, looking at her friend through narrowed eyes, "what have you done now?"

"Why does it always have to be something I've done?" Georgia replied, feigning innocence, "it could have been Khloe or Sage, for that matter, that did whatever it was."

"It's 100% something you did," Millie said, shaking her head at her best friend, "nine times out of ten, it's you!"

"That may be true," Georgia replied before con-tinuing, "the room and bathroom are all messed up, but I wasn't the only one who messed it up."

Millie didn't say anything; to be fair, she wasn't surprised either. She'd shared rooms with all these girls before and knew how messy and disorganized they were. It was lucky that she wasn't friends with them because of how neat and organized they were.

She just sighed, "it's okay. I expect no less. Besides, housekeeping will clean it up when we're touring the city today."

"Oh yeah," Georgia replied, "I forgot about that. Normally we're not staying anywhere long enough for housekeeping. That's awesome! Patty, what are we doing today?" Georgia said, switching to Millie's mom.

"Well, once everyone has eaten breakfast and gotten ready, we're going to meet some of the Swedish girls. I think that Alice, Astrid, and Ella will be coming with us today. What else? Oh yes, we're going on a bus, and you'll have to wait and find out where we are going."

"Boo," Georgia shouted, "no fair! I'm sure it'll be great."

Millie looked around the dining room at everyone looking at them. *Yes, they definitely think we're a little weird.*

"Millie!" Astrid and Alice shouted when they saw her, rushing up to their long-distance friend from Dakota.

Millie had hosted both twins when they had come to Dakota for their International Festival games. Ever since, the girls had all stayed in touch, talking or texting almost daily.

The girls had all walked the short distance from the hotel to a large square. Neither the coaches nor Millie's mom had told them what they were doing, and now they were all just waiting around and snapping photos with their cameras and phones.

"It's so cool to see you!" Millie shouted back, hugging the twins, "your country is so beautiful."

"I told you that it would be," Alice said confidently. Of the two sisters, Alice was definitely the more outgoing and bubbly, with her sister Astrid being the quiet, shy one, which made it all the funnier that Astrid had developed a crush on Cameron when the sisters were in Dakota.

"How is my Cameron?" Astrid said, looking around as if he was about to pop out from behind a bush. "You didn't bring him?"

"No," Georgia said laughing, "he'd just stink up our room and spend the whole trip making gooey puppy dog eyes at you anyway!"

"She's right!" Alice laughed, "like we want to watch the two of you giving each other smooches and holding hands the whole trip!"

"We wouldn't," Astrid said blushing, her fair complexion going bright red, "we're just friends anyway." While Cameron and Astrid had developed a crush on each other, they knew it would never survive the massive distance between them, but they remained close friends.

Ella, the senior Swedish goalie, had also come along. She and Khloe ran across the square and jumped into each other's arms like long-lost sisters, spinning each other round and round.

"Goalies, right?" Georgia said, shrugging her shoulders as if that was the only explanation needed. Khloe had hosted both the Swedish goalies, Ella and Alma, but Alma didn't live in Stockholm and couldn't come into the city for the tour.

"Everyone gather round, please, and listen up," Coach Phil said, shouting so that he could be heard over the bustling sounds of the city. "Sophia has very kindly come along with some of the Swedish girls to host us on our first tour of the city. Now, we're currently at Tegelbacken. Am I saying that right?"

"Close," Coach Sophia said, laughing, "an excellent try. To start our tour, we will be getting on one of those large red double-decker buses you may have already seen driving around the city. So, once it arrives, we'll jump on, and they'll take us around the city.

Their first stop, where they would spend a large part of their first day in Stockholm, would be in Old Town or Gamla Stan, consisting of Stadsholmen island and the islets of Riddarholmen, Helgeandsholmen, and Strömsborg and was the original city of Stockholm. It was home to beautiful, cobbled streets, seventeenth and eighteenth century buildings, Storkyrkan Cathedral, and Royal Palace, the king's official residence.

"This place is amazing," Millie said to Astrid, Alice, and Georgia, "none of the buildings back home look anything like this."

"The Royal Palace and the Royal Chapel were so cool," Georgia added, "imagine what this place looks like at night. It would be so beautiful with the different colored buildings lit up."

"It's pretty special," Alice replied, "I've been here a few times at night with my parents. They put different colored lights up on the buildings and those little twinkly lights all over the trees and stuff. It's awesome."

The girls had all gotten off the bus and broken up into smaller groups, with one of the coaches or

Millie's mom going with each group as they went to different areas around Gamla Stan. After seeing the more significant attractions, they all met back up in the central square to have lunch at one of the many cafés around the area.

"Do you guys know where we're going next?" Georgia asked the two Swedish sisters, "the coaches haven't told us anything."

The two sisters shared a knowing look but motioned as if their lips were sealed.

"I knew you two would know!" Georgia said, frustrated, "and you won't tell us? That's no fun. If Lily were here, she totally would have told me by now." Lily was the Swedish girl who stayed with Georgia when the girls visited Dakota.

"Probably," Astrid said laughing, "she is terrible at keeping secrets, but she's not here, so you'll need to wait and see!"

As it turned out, Georgia wouldn't have to wait long as it was almost time to board the bus again for the day's last stop.

"How did everyone enjoy Gamla Stan?" Coach Sophia asked when the group had all sat down on the tour bus. She was talking over the microphone as half the group was seated upstairs and half downstairs. "Our next stop will be the ICEBAR, so I hope you all brought your winter jackets!"

"An ice bar?" Georgia whispered to Millie, "surely she's joking?"

"I guess we'll find out!" Millie replied, curious herself about what Coach Sophia meant.

"This place is so cool!" Sage said as she sipped her frozen drink, "but I wouldn't want to stay here for very long. It's seriously freezing."

"It's an ice bar. If it were warm, the whole place would melt, silly," Georgia said, laughing, "then it would be a pool bar!"

The Stockholm ICEBAR was made entirely of ice, and even the drinks the girls were drinking were served in glasses made entirely of ice. The bar was kept at a constant temperature of 23°F and could fit sixty people at a time.

When they arrived at ICEBAR, each girl was given a warm coat and gloves to wear while inside.

"It's pretty cool," Millie agreed, "but imagine working here all day? They must be frozen half to death."

"We should show Mr. Rossi back at the restaurant a photo of this place," Khloe added, "and the cooks. They wouldn't be able to complain about how hot the kitchen was if they worked here."

Khloe's comment had all the kids laughing, and Georgia had to explain to Astrid, Alice, and Ella how they had raised money for the trip by working in Mr. Rossi's Italian restaurant for the night and how hot it had been for the girls in the kitchen.

The girls finished their frozen drinks and piled back onto the bus for the quick trip back to the hotel, where they said goodbye to the Swedish girls for the day.

"So," Millie's mom said as she addressed the girls later that night in the large room where they all gathered for pizza and pasta, "how did you all enjoy your first day in Stockholm?"

There were many tired-looking girls nodding and saying how great it was, but jet lag had finally kicked in for most of the group, and most of the girls were half asleep as they ate their dinner.

"Well, we'll take that as a yes," Coach Phil said yawning, "I don't know about y'all, but I'm tired and ready for bed, so let's call it a night. We have a big day again tomorrow, so grab some rest."

"ARE YOU COMING downstairs for a swim?" Lola asked, poking her head into Millie's room. As they were all staying as a group, the hotel had grouped them on one floor at the end of the hallway. Most of the girls kept their doors open while they were at the hotel and had been walking in and out of each other's rooms to hang out.

"Khloe and Sage aren't," Millie shouted back from the bedroom, "but Georgia and I are. Gimme like two minutes to get changed."

"S'up, Lola?" Georgia said, coming out of the bathroom in her bathing suit, "are you ready to get your swim on?"

"I sure am," Lola replied, spinning around, "Dad said it'll help us get over the jet lag a little faster too. A bit of exercise and all that, you know.

Is she really going to be ready in a minute?" Lola asked doubtfully.

All the girls knew Millie was never on time and probably the least organized on the team.

"Oh, she's probably in our room cleaning," Georgia said laughing, "this is the new Millie. She's a lean, mean cleaning machine. Oh, and she's super organized too."

"Who's mean and organized?" Millie said, coming out of her room and catching the tail end of Georgia and Lola's conversation.

"Nobody," Lola said, winking at Georgia, "let's go swimming!"

"Are there special Swedish sandwiches?" Cameron asked, as he spoke to Millie on the video chat.

"Special Swedish what?" Millie asked, confused and looking at the sandwich in her hand, "what are you talking about?"

"I just thought you might be eating some fancy sandwiches or something because you were in Sweden," Cameron said laughing.

"Cameron," Millie said, "how long have you known me?"

"A long time," Cameron replied, "maybe too long," already guessing what her following comment would be by her tone.

"And in that time," Millie said slowly as if she was explaining something to a tiny child, "have you ever seen me eat anything strange or exotic?"

"No," Cameron said, "so I'm guessing it's probably ham and cheese or peanut butter and jelly."

"Ham and cheese," Millie said, "apparently, they were out of peanut butter."

"Besides the lack of peanut butter," Cameron said laughing, "how is Sweden? I know you've only been there a day or so, but have you done anything cool yet?"

"Oh yeah, it feels like it's going so quick already," Millie answered, "but we got to do some sightseeing yesterday. We went to this place called Gamla Stan and got to walk through the Royal Palace and Royal Cathedral. Then we went to ICEBAR, this bar and restaurant made totally out of ice. Even the glasses we drank out of were made from ice. So, it was pretty cool."

"Wow," Cameron replied, "that sounds so cool. Is it bedtime there? Why is your hair all wet?"

"What, are you a detective?" Millie laughed, "we just went swimming in the hotel pool, and I just jumped out of the shower. We have our first practice this afternoon," Millie answered before filling in some more about their day sightseeing with Astrid, Alice, and Ella, as well as some of the other sights they'd seen on their tour through the city.

"This place is epic!" Georgia said, as she stopped on the ice close to where Millie was adjusting her helmet.

The girls had finished their lunch at the hotel, then got picked up by a bus, which took them across the city to the arena. It was about a thirty-minute trip through the center of Stockholm and considering traffic, not a bad journey at all. It had also given the girls more of an opportunity to look at the city and take photos along the way through the large windows of the bus.

"Let's go, let's go!" Coach Phil shouted from the center of the arena, "we only have about two hours, so I want to make the most of it. Tomorrow will be the first day of the tournament, so this is the only opportunity we could get to practice. We were lucky enough for Coach Sophia to pull some strings and get us the ice time."

Coach Sophia knew the management team at the arena because of her job for Team Sweden, so she had called in some favors to squeeze the

Hurricanes into the schedule so they could have at least one skate before the tournament.

The girls were slow getting ready and slow hitting the ice, and Coach Phil was getting a little bit annoyed about it, the frustration clearly visible on his face.

"It's the jetlag," Coach Sophia said, as she skated up to him, "they're not used to traveling halfway around the world. Even my girls that travel around Europe a lot for tournaments for Team Sweden were rough when they flew to America."

"You're probably right," Coach Phil replied, "it's probably why I'm so cranky too. I keep forgetting about jetlag."

"They'll all be fine by tomorrow," Coach Sophia replied, "just have them get a decent sleep tonight again and drink lots of water."

"Will do," Coach Phil said, "and thanks again for arranging this ice time. It's very much appreciated."

"Please, after everything you guys did for us when we came to Dakota, it's the least I can do. So let's go and see if we can get those tired old ladies out there moving!"

"Seriously, my legs hurt in places that I didn't think was possible," Georgia said, as she lay on the bed next to Millie in their shared room.

"My muscles have sore muscles," Khloe added from the lounge area, "goalies shouldn't have to skate that much."

"I thought earlier, you told us *'goalies are built different,'* isn't that, right?" Sage said, as she made little quotation marks in the air over her head, "how's that working out?"

"That was before Coach Sophia made me do a hundred laps of the arena," Khloe whined, "now, more than ever, I'm glad I chose to be a goalie. I'm happy I don't normally have to skate that much!" It wasn't that Khloe wasn't fit, but as a goalie, she didn't usually have to do all the same drills the players did. However, Coach Sophia was a coach for Team Sweden, and she expected her goalies to do as much work as all the other players.

"Anyway, I'm taking a nap for an hour before dinner," Millie said, "we have that hockey game after dinner, and I don't want to be yawning all night."

The rest of the girls agreed, heading to their rooms to try and sneak in a quick nap before dinner.

"Okay, ladies," Millie's mom said, "let's wrap up dinner and head outside. The bus is here to take us to the arena."

All the girls and coaches had been fortunate enough to secure tickets to watch Team Sweden play Team Finland at the Avicii Arena. Coach Sophia had come through in a big way for the girls on this trip.

It was only a quick trip to the arena, and Coach Sophia was there to meet them at the entrance and get them through security and into their assigned seats, going through the coach and player's entrances. They'd even seen some of the Team Sweden girls warming up along the way!

Once seated, Millie leaned over and gave Georgia a little nudge, "and you thought that the arena we were in this morning was big!"

The girls barely took their eyes off the ice and the game in front of them for the remainder of the game. Coach Sophia had come over after the first period and given them a bunch of Swedish flags so that they could support the team, and they'd been waving and cheering like crazy ever since.

"This has been the coolest game," Violet said, "even though we're not Swedish, I kind of feel like I'm a little bit Swedish now."

"Same," Lola replied, "I think we have to support our friend's country."

"I hope they can hold this lead for a few more minutes," Sage added, "they deserve it."

The girls from Team Sweden had taken a strong lead in the first period, finishing 2–0, but Team Finland had managed to keep them scoreless in the second period and come out strong in the third, scoring one goal to bring the score to 2–1 heading into the final few minutes of the game.

"Let's go, Team Sweden!" Khloe shouted from behind them, joining in with some new Swedish friends she'd made in the stands.

With only a minute and a half left on the clock, Team Finland called a time-out.

"They have to go for it now," Lola said, "all or nothing in the last minute."

"For sure," Millie replied, "that goalie will be ready to hit the bench hard if they get the puck up into their forward area."

Just like the girls had predicted, the second the puck cleared the center line, the Finnish goalie hit the bench so fast Khloe's jaw dropped. "Now I know why Coach Sophia has all her goalies skating so much," she said, impressed.

Despite having the extra player on the ice, the Swedish girls kept the puck away from the goalie long enough for the timer to tick down and the final siren to buzz.

"That was a cool game," Georgia said softly to Millie as they lay in bed back in the hotel.

"I know, right?" Millie replied, "one day, I hope I'm playing for my country like those girls."

"It would be so epic," Georgia answered, "out there playing in front of such a massive crowd."

"Right?" Millie said, "it would be so awesome, but I can barely keep my eyes open right now. I have to sleep."

"Same. I don't think I've ever been this tired in my whole life. Night, Mills," Georgia said, before yawning and rolling over."

"Night, Georgia," Millie replied, getting her pillow comfortable and shutting her eyes.

Both girls were asleep within minutes.

Tomorrow would be the first day of their tournament, and it would be a big one.

"OKAY, I THINK I'm done with jet lag," Millie's mom said to her and the other girls over breakfast, "I'm glad I don't have to travel around the world for work." All four girls had come downstairs to join Millie's mom for her early breakfast today.

"We all woke up a lot better today," Sage replied, "and I already cleaned up, called Mom and Dad, and cleaned my room. So I feel, like fresher? Or something."

"Same," Millie replied, "I called Dad, and he was busy cleaning."

"That's a big lie, Millie," her mom said, shaking her head, "I know your dad, and he's 100% going to leave any cleaning until the last minute. Plus, we share a bank account, and I can see all the junk food he's eating."

"Maybe," Millie replied, "but he told me to tell you he was cleaning up!"

"That sounds more like your dad," Millie's mom said, laughing, "and closer to the truth."

"How long until we have to leave, Mrs. Duncan?" Khloe asked.

"I told you to call me Patty already, Khloe. Mrs. Duncan is my mother, and you're making me feel old. Coach Phil told me that the first game is at eleven, so we want to be at the arena by nine thirty and on the bus by nine o'clock. So, about thirty minutes or so."

"That's perfect," Khloe replied, getting up from the table, "I'll go call my parents and get ready!"

"Okay, girls, the first team we're facing in the tournament is Ishundar. I think I said that right. Oh, it says underneath in brackets the Ice Dogs. I asked Coach Sophia about all the teams, and apparently, these guys are at the bottom end of the rankings, so this will be a good way for us to gauge where we stand." Coach Phil was reading from his notes as he talked to the girls.

Coach Sophia, the other coaches, and he had all spent a few hours last night looking at some highlights of the other teams, going over strategy, and working out which teams would be the biggest challenge.

"So, let's set the pace early in this game and let everyone know we're serious and here to win! Let's go, Hurricanes!"

"Hurricanes! Hurricanes! Hurricanes!" The girls all shouted while banging their sticks up and down before making their way out onto the ice for the tournament's first game.

After a quick warm-up, the girls lined up on the ice to listen to the national anthem before they split up, with the starting line hitting their spots and the rest of the team heading for the benches.

Millie was nervous, but surprisingly, not as nervous as she expected she would be considering the size of the crowd and the arena and playing in her first international tournament. Playing on the State Team last year had really taught her a lot and really boosted her confidence, both on and off the ice.

"Players ready?" the ref asked, looking at both the centers. Millie and the other girl nodded.

"Goalies ready? she asked, holding up the puck and looking at each team's goalie. Both Khloe and the other goalie nodded, and the ref blew her whistle, dropping the puck. Game on!

Millie and the other center both dived for the puck, but Millie won the first face-off and came away with the puck, immediately skating backward in a large circle, giving her forwards time to get into position.

Georgia quickly outskated her opponent, pushing forward to intercept the puck Millie sent flying her way. Picking up the puck cleanly, she faked out the defense player skating towards her before continuing up the ice, looking to her left and right to see where Violet was.

Violet was clear, slapping her stick on the ice and calling for the puck, so Georgia sent it flying towards her across the ice. Picking up the puck cleanly, Violet held it long enough for Georgia to clear her defender, then sent it back.

Georgia didn't even wait for the puck to stop, pulling her stick back and connecting with the puck in a powerful slap shot that sent the puck sailing toward the top right corner of the net.

Goal! Despite the goalie's best efforts to track the puck, the transition from Violet to Georgia and the speed and power of the slap shot had been too much. She'd reacted just a second too slow to stop the shot.

Georgia and the other girls from her line had scored off the first play. After a quick skate by

the bench for fist bumps, they swapped with the second line.

Their first game was off to a flying start!

"That first goal was a killer, Georgia," Isabelle said, as they sat eating their lunch after the first game, "she never even saw that puck until it was in the net!"

"Thanks," Georgia replied, "I knew it was going in once I felt how I connected with it. Not a doubt!"

The girls had beaten the Ice Dogs 4–1, and the only goal they gave up was because a puck deflected off Averie's skate and bounced back into their net.

"Averie," Khloe said, looking over to where Averie was sitting by herself, "come and sit with us."

"Are you sure? I didn't think you would be too happy with me," Averie replied a little sadly. As one of the younger girls, she didn't get as much ice time, and it wasn't sitting well with her to have scored against her own team.

"Of course," Khloe replied, "I wouldn't have asked if I wasn't being serious, and one other thing, don't worry about the goal. Okay? It happens more than you think. If I got upset at everyone who kicked a puck in my net, I wouldn't have many friends on this team."

"She's right," Georgia added, "I've done it like two or three times at least, and I'm not even down that end very often."

"At least ten times here," Ashlyn added, "it's one of the prices of playing defense. It's just bad luck."

"Thanks," Averie replied, "it just sucks, you know?"

"Yeah," Millie added, "it's like missing important shots at the other end. Game-winning shots. We're not perfect,"

"Speak for yourself," Georgia chimed in, "I'm fairly close. Now, let's go and watch Astrid and Alice play and cheer them on."

"And look for weaknesses," Khloe added, getting horrified looks from the other girls. "What? I just said what y'all are thinking. They might be in a different pool at the moment, but if their team is as good as we think it is, we'll be playing them sooner than you think!"

"What are Khloe and Ella doing?" Coach Phil asked Millie as she skated up to the bench at the end of the second period.

"Oh, they've been doing that all game," Millie laughed, "they do a little bow and then bump blockers."

"I...never mind," Coach Phil said, scratching his head under his cap, "It's locked at 2–2. I think that we'll run with your main line as much as possible for the final period. Have you seen anything that you think we can take advantage of?"

"Their left side is definitely slower," Millie began, "but we've gone that way a lot. Every time I push up the left now, they collapse in on me and close it up."

"What do you think about doubling down on the left attempts and trying to break through? Then, if we haven't got anywhere with that in the first ten minutes, we'll do a left fake, pull Khloe, and throw Kiera out on the ice and have her swing right?" Coach Phil said as he drew it on the small whiteboard he carried.

"I think it'll work," Millie agreed, "but it will only work once. After that, if she misses the shot, they'll be all over us if we try the same play again."

"Only has to work once, Mills," Georgia said, listening in, "just once."

"That's the plan then, girls. Millie, let your line know when you want to do the switch, probably around the five-minute mark, and give me a nod so I can shuffle the girls on the bench."

The girls kept pushing left on all three lines, trying to muscle their way through the Wolves defense, but so far, they hadn't come close to getting a shot on Ella. At the other end, because of the strong offensive plays, Khloe had been under extreme pressure, barely managing to scramble back up to stop a second shot after she went low to block the first.

After the Wolves called a time-out, Millie skated back onto the ice with the rest of her line and looked at the clock. Three minutes left in the game. She gave Khloe a slight nod, barely perceptible to anyone else, and at the same time, did the same to the bench. Coach Phil and some other coaches stood up, blocking the front of the bench, and quickly moved Kiera to the forward gate, and at the same time, Khloe casually moved a few feet out of her crease before getting into her stance.

Millie took the faceoff, won the puck, and, just like the previous plays this period, pushed hard to the left with Georgia right behind her. Like the last few times, the Wolves defense started to collapse onto the two girls pushing up the ice, but in the background, they hadn't noticed that Khloe was halfway to the bench already, skating as if her life depended on it.

The second Khloe hit the bench, Kiera took off through the forward door, skating hard up the right side of the ice.

Seeing the movement, Millie dropped the puck behind her to Georgia, who picked it up and flicked it to Violet, who was skating up the center of the ice. Violet took the puck cleanly and sent it to the right, where Kiera picked it up on the boards and headed straight for Ella.

Ella had seen what was developing, and despite screaming at her defense to drop back, she knew it was too late. She was going to have to face the player coming in alone and started to shift left and right in her crease, trying to anticipate where the shot was going to come in all the time, making herself as big as possible.

For Kiera, time had slowed down. The noise from the players and crowd screaming had faded into the background. Instead, she was 100% focused on Ella standing between her and the net. A player was coming in from her left, but she wouldn't be fast enough to block her shot, so she ignored her.

As she got to within twenty to thirty feet of the net, she pulled her stick back as if going for the slap shot but kept closing in on the net at full speed.

Ella was now frantically moving left to right in front of the net, with no idea where the shot would come from.

Kiera started to swing her stick forward, skating towards the left of the net, but as she saw Ella flinch and start to move to block the shot, she stopped her swing, darted right, and poked the puck to the right of the goalie's leg and into the back of the net. *Goal!*

"Let's have three cheers for Khloe and Kiera!" Coach Phil shouted at dinner that night back in the hotel conference room. Khloe and Kiera had both been awarded player of the match, Kiera for her game-winning goal, and Khloe for her defense throughout the game.

The Wolves had come back hard in the game's final two minutes but hadn't managed to get another goal, and the final score had been 3–2 for the Hurricanes.

Millie's mom and the coaches ordered all the kids burgers and fries from a local burger restaurant to celebrate dinner for winning their first two games.

After the cheering and clapping had stopped, Coach Phil started to talk again. "Great start, girls. Two good wins, and now we just have one more game in the morning before the quarterfinals. So, once you've eaten, you can go for a swim if you want, but just relax. No playing around, and then it's into rooms by 9:00 p.m. for an early night."

The Hurricanes had already beaten two teams, but they still had a long and challenging journey to make it to the final game.

"OKAY, WE LOST that game. But, it's not the end of the world," Coach Phil said to the Hurricanes in the changeroom after the game. "The Wolverines are possibly one of the best, if not the best, teams in this tournament, and the way they've been playing, if we make it through the next few games, we could be playing against them again. We have a few hours now to rest and grab some lunch, so I want all of you to drink lots of water, eat something healthy, and forget about this morning's game. We'll meet up half an hour earlier than usual and talk through this game with clear heads."

The girls had tried their best, but their luck hadn't been with them this morning. Unfortunately, losing wasn't something any of them took easily. Therefore, it was a group of disappointed girls who headed out of the changeroom and off towards the cafeteria.

"That was a rough game," Coach Phil said, sitting down with Millie's mom, Coach Sophia, and the other Hurricanes coaches, "no other way to cut it."

"The girls all played well," Coach Sophia began sipping her coffee, "the Wolverines are just bigger and better. Now that they've made it through to the semifinals, they'll be playing against the better teams in the Tournament."

"Is there anything we can focus on for the next games?" Millie's mom asked. Typically, she wouldn't have been at this coach's meeting, but as she had come on the trip instead of Janet, the team manager, and she was the only parent there, Coach Phil had invited her to all the meetings with the other coaches.

"Honestly," Coach Sophia answered her, "I don't think so. The girls are good, especially Millie, Georgia, Khloe, and the twins that play defense," which made Coach Phil grin, "it's just a size and speed thing with teams like the Wolverines. Your team is a good mix of juniors and seniors, but the Wolverines and others don't have any juniors."

"No weaker lines," one of the other coaches said, agreeing with her.

"Exactly. So, instead of having maybe like one or two strong lines like you guys, they have three strong lines that they can continually keep rotating in and out of the game," Coach Sophia said.

"So, we placed second in our pool, which means that we're heading to the quarterfinals next, and the Wolverines who placed first get a bye, correct?" Coach Phil said, looking at the tablet, which was updated by the tournament with their brackets. Most of it was in Swedish, so Coach Sophia had been translating for them.

"Yeah, they go straight into the semifinals. But, yeah, they won't play again today, so they'll be that much fresher when they play tomorrow," Coach Sophia replied.

The coaches and Millie's mom spent the next hour trying to come up with some plays that might give them an edge over some of these bigger teams they'd be facing, including the Red Eagles and possibly Astrid and Alice's team, the Bears.

"Time-out!" Khloe shouted at the bench to get the coach's attention, "call a time-out!"

One of the other coaches noticed, tapped Coach Phil on the arm, and told him Khloe was asking for a time-out.

"Ref! Can we get a time-out?" Coach Phil shouted, getting the ref's attention.

The referee blew her whistle, stopping the game while all the players skated to their respective benches.

"What's up, Khloe?" Then, as she approached the bench, Coach Phil asked, "your gear needs adjusting?"

"No," Khloe puffed, "I need a drink, and I want to know why we're letting them line up against me and just take shots like they're training."

The girls had dominated the first two periods of their quarterfinal game against the Red Eagles, quickly piling on four unanswered goals. Still, since the start of the third period, they had been coasting, and the score was now 4–2, with Khloe coming under mounting pressure.

"It sucks, I know," Coach Phil explained, "but whatever team we play in the morning, they would have had most of today to rest. It's elimination from here on out, so goals against won't matter, and I'm trying to rest the first two lines as much as possible. I know you're getting hammered out there, but if we can rest as much as possible, we'll have some gas left in the tank tomorrow. Does that make sense?"

"It does," Khloe said, understanding the idea behind it but not liking it one little bit, "it just felt like we were letting them skate in and take shots at me, is all."

"We'll do better, Khloe," Maize said, "they're just big, is all."

"Yeah, okay. As long as it's better for the team, I can handle it, Coach," Khloe said, taking a fresh water bottle and slipping her helmet back on.

"Thanks, Khloe," Coach Phil said, giving her a fist bump, "if they score one more, I'll swap the third line out for the first line."

"Roger!" Khloe shouted, "let's go, Hurricanes!"

"Let's go, Hurricanes!" All the girls shouted back before returning to the ice for the game's final minutes.

"Hey, ladies!" Ella shouted when she, Alice, and Astrid walked into the hotel lobby later that afternoon, "is this dinner to make up for that sneaky stunt you pulled out on the ice yesterday?"

Alice, Astrid, and Ella were coming to hang out for the evening at the hotel, have dinner, and have a quick soak in the hotel spa and pool with the girls.

"I don't know what you're talking about?" Khloe said, shrugging her shoulders, "we don't do sneaky."

"Please," Ella said laughing, "don't try and trick a trickster. You guys must have Loki himself on your bench to have pulled off that play!"

Ella explained to Astrid and Alice what the girls had done, pulling Khloe off the ice and scoring against her to win the game. Astrid and Alice laughed and quickly explained to the Dakota girls that Loki was the brother of Thor, son of Odin, and according to Norse mythology, was the trickster of the group.

"Don't try that against us in the morning," Alice said laughing, "we're wise to you, Hurricanes, now!"

"I can't believe that we're playing you guys tomorrow," Millie said, "of all the teams in the tournament, we had to get you in the semifinals."

"It could be worse," Georgia said, "we could have been playing those Wolverines again."

"The Wolverines are the best tournament team in Sweden," Ella said, "they absolutely destroyed us in our first game."

"She's right," Alice explained, "they're like what you would call a professional tournament team. The kids on that team all go to a special school or hockey academy. They don't even play on Team Sweden until they get to the next age group up as they think it takes away too much from their tournament schedule."

"That's crazy," Millie said, "no wonder they're so tough to beat, plus they all look so big."

"Yeah, no juniors, it's just seniors on all three lines," Ella said, "anyway, enough about the Wolverines. What's for dinner?"

"Good luck tomorrow," Millie said to Astrid and Alice as they soaked in the spa.

"Good luck to you guys as well," Alice said, "Coach Sophia can't believe how well you're doing in the tournament, considering some of the teams you've played."

"Yeah," Ella agreed, "even with your sneaky play, you guys didn't give up for one minute during our game and deserved to win. My coach was impressed, but she said we shouldn't be too surprised. North America has some of the best hockey players in the world, so it makes sense that you girls would be as good as us."

"We try our best to impress," Georgia said laughing, "us little small-town Dakota girls."

"It's almost time to head home, girls," Coach Sophia said, poking her head into the pool room, "I'll meet you downstairs in ten minutes."

"Boo!" the girls shouted, but they knew they all had a big game in the morning, and a good night's sleep could make all the difference for both teams.

After they got dried and changed, they gave each other a quick hug and said goodnight.

"See you in the morning, Hurricanes!" Astrid shouted.

"Right back at you, Bears!" Georgia shouted in return, with all the girls laughing.

"YOU GIRLS ARE doing great out there," Coach Phil said at the end of the second period. So far, both the Bears and the Hurricanes had gone back and forth, but neither team had managed to get a score on the board.

Even without Astrid or Alice, the Bears were a solid team, and they were almost unbeatable with the two Team Sweden players. The fact that they hadn't been able to score against them showed just how well the Hurricanes were playing and holding their own against the other team. However, the Hurricanes hadn't been able to score yet, either.

"Don't worry about what they're doing out there. We're just going to keep playing our game. We apply pressure, and if or when they make a mistake, we take advantage. I know you're all tired, but we just have to get through the next ten minutes or so. Don't think about what happens next. Just focus on this game. Play your position and follow the plan. Let's go, Hurricanes!"

"Let's go, Hurricanes!" the girls shouted back before Millie, Georgia, and the rest of the first line headed back onto the ice.

"You look tired, Mills," Astrid said in the center of the ice, "you should take an extra minute to rest!"

"Please," Millie replied, "I could play another hour, but if you need a rest, feel free."

Astrid laughed and shook her head. Both girls were exhausted, but neither was about to admit it.

The ref made sure all the players were ready, both goalies, then blew her whistle and dropped the puck.

The final period was under way!

The first ten minutes of the final period went much like the first two, with both teams going back and forth until Georgia cut through the Bears' defenders, took a wild shot at the goal, and bounced the puck into the net off the back of the goalie's shins.

Goal! It was an ugly goal, more luck than skill, but the Hurricanes would take it, and the bench went wild! It was 1–0 for the Hurricanes with less than five minutes left. All they had to was hold on.

However, luck was a fickle thing, and they were about to be on the wrong end of it.

Astrid and Alice weren't about to roll over and give up, and with Isabelle coming in to play center for the second line, they pounced.

Isabelle won the puck on the faceoff but lost it while trying to pass across the ice to Lola, with Astrid swooping in to pick up the puck.

Astrid flicked it to her sister Alice, and the pair fell into position along with their teammates before moving forward. The sisters swiftly broke through the Hurricanes' forwards, immediately throwing them on the defensive in the middle of their line change.

To makes matters worse, as Aniyah and Emma came off the ice to swap with Ashlyn and Daylyn, the door got jammed, and they couldn't get onto the bench. As both girls tried to throw themselves over the top of the gate, Ashlyn and Daylyn had to wait before they could get onto the ice; otherwise, they'd be penalized for having too many players on at once.

With Astrid and Alice already through the forwards, Khloe knew that she was in a world of trouble. She'd played against both sisters when they were in Dakota, and one was bad enough, let alone two of them skating at her.

Despite trying her best, a quick back-and-forth with the puck between the two sisters was all it took to get Khloe out of position and for Astrid to flick the puck into the back of the net.

The score was now 1–1, with less than thirty seconds on the clock. Both teams tried their best to score, but the final siren sounded, and it would now go to sudden death overtime.

Three minutes into the sudden death overtime, with neither team scoring, Millie was taken down hard from behind when one of the Bears players hooked her skate with her stick as she was skating forward. Accident or not, the ref called a penalty, and now they would have an extra player on the ice for two minutes.

"Are you okay, Millie?" Coach Phil asked when she skated to the bench, "are you good to stay on?"

"Yes, Coach," Millie said between gritted teeth. There was no way she wouldn't be going back out on the ice. Injured or otherwise.

"Okay, line one, you're up. Let's use this time well. Khloe, when you see us hit their blue line, you hit this bench, and Kiera, be ready to go. There's no need to try and be sneaky this time. They'll be waiting for us to do it. So let's get out there and win this game!" Coach Phil said, sending his strongest line back onto the ice for the penalty.

They wouldn't have it all their way, though. The Bears put their best penalty-kill team on the ice. They wouldn't make it easy on the Hurricanes.

The ref dropped the puck. Millie won the faceoff and quickly flicked the puck over to where Violet was waiting on the boards. There was no-one covering her. Violet didn't wait long before pushing forward into the corner of the ice. It gave Khloe the opportunity she had been waiting for. She quickly skated to the bench. Kiera tore onto the ice as their sixth player.

Astrid, Alice, and the Bears' two best defensive players were running an amazingly strong box formation, forcing the Hurricanes to pass it back and forth, trying to draw them out. The Bears' penalty kill team knew precisely what they were doing, darting out, disrupting a pass, and putting pressure on the Hurricanes, but never straying far from their defensive zone.

With only thirty seconds of the penalty left, Coach Phil called a time-out and got the girls back to the bench.

"Look, that's one of the best penalty kill lines you'll ever play against, and you're doing exactly what they want you to do, passing it around and wasting time. But you have to take a chance. If we do nothing, we're just back to square one. So, get out there and get it done. Let's go!" Coach Phil said to Millie's line, sending them back onto the ice again, minus Khloe, who would remain on the bench.

Millie won the puck on the faceoff, quickly passing the puck back to Ashlyn, who came to a stop and pulled her stick back for a slap shot on goal. As the rest of the Hurricanes pushed into the net, the defense collapsed back, but the Hurricanes players kept pushing in with them, trying to screen the shot as it came in.

It was too late, despite the Bears players trying to push the girls out of the way. The Bears' goalie couldn't track the puck as it screamed toward her. The red buzzer sounded, signaling a goal, with most of the players surprised that the puck had gone in. None of them could see it amongst all the pushing and shoving in front of the net.

Ashlyn had just won the game!

Astrid and Alice were the first to approach the girls and shake their hands despite losing.

"Great game!" they said, "you guys are crazy good and just a little bit lucky."

"I feel like we just won the tournament," Millie said, "but it wasn't even the last game!"

"Our coach just told us the Wolverines are winning like 4–1 on the other arena, so you'll be playing them later by the looks of it," Alice said.

"Great!" Kiera said, "just fantastic."

"We have to go and have a meeting and get changed, but we'll meet in the cafeteria for something to eat?" Astrid said to the girls.

"For sure," Millie replied, "see you soon."

"Here you go, girls," Millie's mom said, putting down a bag full of sandwiches, "I know you must be all getting sick of the cafeteria food by now."

"Thanks, Patty," the girls chorused.

"And, great game Alice and Astrid," Millie's mom said, "and you too yesterday, Ella. You're all fortunate to have the skills you have. Okay, I have to make sure the rest of the girls have all had something to eat. Millie, remember to be back at the changeroom by 1:00 p.m. Your final game is at 2:00 p.m."

"Yes, Mom," Millie replied, "I won't be late."

"Your mom is so sweet," Astrid said after she left, "you must be glad to have her on the trip with you."

"It really is cool," Millie replied, "I think it would have been so much stressful flying around the world without her there."

"When we flew to America to stay with you, it was pretty tense at times, but we'd already been traveling around Europe and dealing with customs and borders and stuff, so that made it a little less scary," Alice said, "but if it were the first time, it would have been scarier for sure. So, it was more like just a longer trip than usual."

"Great game, by the way," Astrid said. "Really, our coach was upset that we didn't win, but she said that she was so impressed by you guys and to tell you good luck against the Wolverines this afternoon."

"Thanks," Millie replied, "but I think we've just about used up all our luck for this trip!"

Millie's premonition was to prove correct. The Hurricanes had used up all their luck, going down to the Wolverines in the final game 3–1.

However, after the excitement of the previous game against their friends, the final match felt like an anticlimax, and the girls and their coaches couldn't have been happier.

"THIS IS SUCH a cool place to skate!" Georgia said to Alice and Astrid, "right in the middle of the city. I'm glad we got a chance to see each other and have one last skate that wasn't in an arena."

"I know," Astrid said, "even if it is seven in the morning!"

Because of their busy schedule, and the fact that they'd made it through to the final games, the girls' only opportunity for a skate was early in the morning on the day they were flying home. Millie's mom had walked down with anyone wanting to go, and they had an hour before they had to return to the hotel to finish packing.

Luckily, Alice, Astrid, and Ella had been able to meet them here for a final skate and to say goodbye before they left.

"I thought we'd be the only ones here this early," Violet said, as she skated past, "but there are loads of people."

"People in Sweden love to skate," Ella said, "and to stay active. People come and skate before work and school all the time."

"I'm sorry you guys lost to the Wolverines," Astrid said. "We watched the game. Those girls are just so big and fast."

"Yeah," Georgia replied, "honestly, I don't even mind. It's not fun to lose, but we had so much fun on this trip and got to hang out with you guys and play hockey and skate. I feel like we won anyway."

"She's right," Millie agreed, "maybe our hearts weren't in that last game."

"Maybe," Alice agreed. "I'm going to miss you guys so much! Who knows when we'll be able to hang out again."

"Please," Georgia replied, "when I'm older and rich, I'm coming over here all the time!" The girls laughed and skated around for the rest of the time before hugging goodbye. It was emotional, without a dry eye among them. Who knows what everyone else skating was thinking about a group of girls alternating between hugging, crying, and laughing.

"You'll see them again, Mills," Millie's mom said to Millie, reaching across the plane seat and giving her daughter a big hug.

"You think?" Millie answered as they watched the city of Stockholm getting smaller and smaller below them, "you really think we will?"

"Yes. Life is funny like that sometimes."

"I hope so," Millie said, "I really hope so."

"Dad!" Millie shouted, running up to her father in the baggage claim of the airport, jumping up and giving him a big hug. "It's so good to see you!"

"Jeez," her dad replied, "maybe you need to go away more often if I'm going to get a greeting like this! How was the flight home?"

"Long," his wife replied, "too long, but better now that I'm home. How was your week? Did you enjoy the peace and quiet?"

"It was too quiet," he replied, "and I think I've eaten every type of takeout in town. In fact, I know I have, and I may need to eat salad for the next week."

"We know," Millie replied laughing, "Mom showed me the receipts."

"Millie," Georgia shouted across the baggage area, "I'm going home. I'll text you later if I haven't fallen asleep."

"See you, Georgia," Millie replied, giving her friend a wave.

"Okay," Millie's dad said, picking up their suitcases, "let's get you home so you can relax."

"It better be spotless," Millie's mom said laughing, "I'm too tired to clean."

"Umm," Millie's dad said, winking at Millie, "it's pretty clean!"

"Brian, so help me," Millie's mom said, rolling her eyes and walking off, "I'm too tired for your jokes."

"Millie!" her mom shouted from downstairs after dinner, "Cameron is here."

"Coming!" Millie shouted, dragging herself off the bed, throwing on a sweater, and heading downstairs.

"Welcome home," Cameron said when she walked into the room, "Mom wouldn't let me come to the airport, said I had to let you 'settle in,' whatever that means," making air quotes.

"Nah, you should have come," Millie said, "it would have given me someone to talk to on the way home."

"I was in the car," Millie's dad said, "like physically in the car with you the whole ride home."

"True," Millie began, "but you and Mom were chatting. Let's go down to the basement and hang out."

The two of them went downstairs to the basement, turning the TV on. Millie lay on the couch, and Cameron grabbed a hockey stick and started flicking the puck up and down.

"You finally learned that trick, huh?" Millie replied, "it took you long enough!"

The End.

Stay Tuned for

Hockey Wars 13

Coming Fall 2023

Made in the USA
Monee, IL
01 May 2025

16730204R00077